FIRE READY

Michelle Vasiliu
Cheryl Orsini

Australia • Brazil • Japan • Korea • Mexico • Singapore • Spain • United Kingdom • United States

Fire Ready

Fast Forward
Emerald Level 25

Text: Michelle Vasiliu
Illustrations: Cheryl Orsini
Editor: Cameron Macintosh
Design: Ami Sharpe
Series design: James Lowe
Production controller: Seona Galbally
Audio recordings: Juliet Hill, Picture Start
Spoken by: Matthew King and Abbe Holmes
Reprint: Jennifer Foo

ISBN 978 0 17 012719 6
ISBN 978 0 17 012717 2 (set)

Cengage Learning Australia
Level 7, 80 Dorcas Street
South Melbourne, Victoria Australia 3205
Phone: 1300 790 853

Cengage Learning New Zealand
Unit 4B Rosedale Office Park
331 Rosedale Road, Albany, North Shore NZ 0632
Phone: 0508 635 766

For learning solutions, visit cengage.com.au

Printed in Australia by Ligare Pty Ltd
6 7 8 9 10 11 12 21 20 19 18 17

Evaluated in independent research by staff from the Department of Language, Literacy and Arts Education at the University of Melbourne.

Contents

Chapter 1

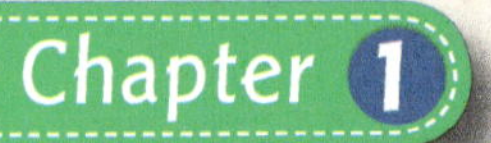

Saturday

The dry sunburnt leaves crackled under Luca's feet. Along the back fence where the forest began, the ferns wilted. Luca picked up the last of the leaves and put them in the bin. As he dropped the metal lid, he checked to make sure it was locked on tightly. Then he wandered towards the cottage where it was cooler.

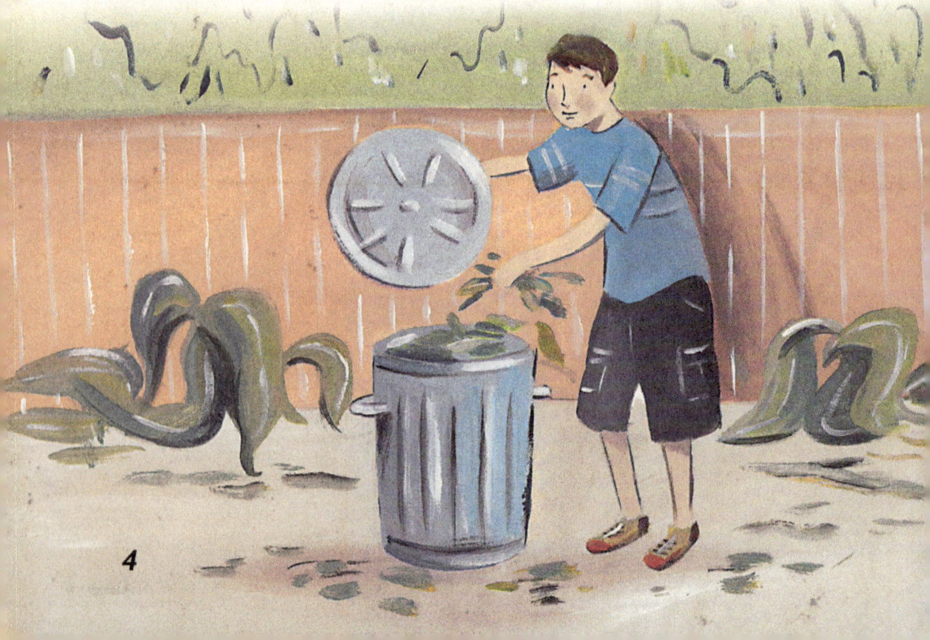

Luca was glad it was Saturday. On weekdays, he spent more than an hour on the bus just getting to school. Most days, he liked riding on the bus. For the first half hour, he was the only passenger. He'd sit and look out the window, the early morning air sweeping through the vents. As the bus wound its way down the mountain, he'd take in the towering trees.

On days like today, though, when the air was hot and sticky, it was a relief not having to make the long bus trip to school.

Luca went to clear away the breakfast dishes. He knew his mum would be tired when she got home. It was her third late shift this week. Now that it was just the two of them, she did a lot of late shifts.

Even after all these months, Luca wasn't used to the silence. He turned on the radio as he cleared the dishes. "Fire-fighters warn spot fires at the base of the mountain may spread," said the announcer.

Luca could feel his heart racing. He went to call his dad, but he stopped, suddenly.

"The CFA advises residents to put their bushfire survival plans into action."

Running Words 261

Luca tried to stay calm. "Mum will be home any minute," he told himself. His heart jumped as the phone rang.

"Darling," came his mother's voice. "They won't let us up the mountain. They say it's much too ..." The line went dead. A moment later, the power cut out.

Chapter 2

Getting Ready

Luca stood in the kitchen and read the list one more time. If he worked through each job like he and his mum had practised, he'd get through this. Dressed in long pants, boots, gloves and a thick woollen top, he went outside.

As Luca blocked the down pipes with gutter plugs, he thought back to the time when he and his mum moved into the cottage. It had been the middle of spring, exactly three months after the accident. Luca remembered how determined his mum had been about being fire ready. With tears in her eyes, she'd told Luca how she wanted to be prepared this time – for anything. Even before they unpacked, she'd insisted on clearing the long grass at the back.

By week two, Luca's mum had organised one of the CFA officers to come around. When the CFA man came by the next day, he talked to Luca and his mum about how they could prepare themselves for the bushfire season. He checked their water tank and pump, and showed them how to burn off safely. He even helped them draw up a bushfire survival plan.

As they sat around the kitchen table and talked about the plan, Luca had looked out into the garden. He'd watched the water drip from the ferns onto the thick green grass, and wondered if the extra work was really necessary.

Luca had gone along with it all anyway. When his mum brought home a roll of metal mesh, he helped her put it on the outside vents. The week after, he helped her put weather stripping on the inside of all the doors and windows. And the week after that, he was there to give her a hand when she put leaf guards over the gutters. He even agreed to do a practice run of the plan.

"Just in case," his mum had said.

Chapter 3

Waiting

Luca was halfway down the ladder when he smelt the smoke. He looked out across the forest. There was a thick dark cloud approaching. With his heart pounding, Luca jumped from the ladder and raced for the back door.

Inside the house, Luca moved quickly. First, he shut all the doors and windows and made sure they were clear of furniture. Next, he took towels and woollen blankets from the hall cupboard and pushed them under all the doors and over the air vents. He filled the bath and sinks with water. He went into the kitchen and grabbed the radio, a torch and some batteries. Then he filled two large water containers and took everything into the living room.

Finally, with the last of the blankets over him, Luca got down low on the floor, and waited.

It was hot and stuffy under the blanket. Luca reached down and found the torch. He turned it on and flashed it over the face of his watch. He'd been there for almost half an hour.

As he wiped the sweat from his brow, he thought about his mum. He remembered her screams that night the hospital called. For hours afterwards, she'd sat, dazed and shocked.

Listening to the fire roar outside, Luca wondered how his mum would cope if she lost him, too.

Luca stood up, and the blanket fell silently to the floor. Now that the main fire front had passed, it was strangely quiet. Luca remembered what the CFA man had said about checking for spot fires. As he took off for the back door, Luca knew he wasn't out of danger yet.

The fire-fighters arrived almost two hours later. Luca was on the ladder, hose in hand. He finished wetting down the house and climbed down from the ladder. Then he walked over to where the fire-fighters were, and helped put out the embers, burning along the back fence where the ferns had been.

Chapter 4

News Reports

For days, the papers were full of it. There was news report after news report, describing how Luca had saved the cottage and himself while his mum took shelter at the local hall.

There were photos too – photos of the charred, leafless trees still smouldering in the ashen dirt, photos of Luca standing outside the blackened cottage, and photos of Luca and his mum, hugging.

Then there was Luca's quote in the paper, too. "Sometimes stuff just happens. There's nothing you can do to change it, and that's hard. But when you're prepared, at least you're in there with a chance."